Jennifer Lawrence

by Sarah Tieck

ABDO
Publishing Company

VISIT US AT
www.abdopublishing.com

Published by ABDO Publishing Company, PO Box 398166, Minneapolis, Minnesota 55439.

Printed in the United States of America, North Mankato, Minnesota.
102012
012013

Coordinating Series Editor: Rochelle Baltzer
Contributing Editors: Stephanie Hedlund, Marcia Zappa
Graphic Design: Maria Hosley
Cover Photograph: *AP Photo*: Joel Ryan.
Interior Photographs/Illustrations: *AP Photo*: Carlo Allegri (p. 9), Suzanne Collins/PR NEWSWIRE (p. 21), Foto AP/The Fort Worth Star-Telegram, Max Faulkner (p. 21), Jennifer Graylock (p. 21), Andrew Medichini (p. 13), Chris Pizzello (p. 29), Rex Features via AP Images (p. 17), Joel Ryan (p. 19), Marcio Jose Sanchez (p. 22), Charles Sykes (p. 24); *Getty Images*: E. Charbonneau/WireImage (p. 11), Murray Close (p. 14), Pablo Blazquez Dominguez/WireImage (p. 5), Juan Naharro Gimenez (p. 23), Pascal Le Segretain (p. 27); *Shutterstock*: Songquan Deng (p. 9), Lisa F. Young (p. 7).

Cataloging-in-Publication Data

Tieck, Sarah.
Jennifer Lawrence: star of the Hunger Games / Sarah Tieck.
p. cm. -- (Big buddy biographies)
ISBN 978-1-61783-751-7
1. Lawrence, Jennifer, 1990- --Juvenile literature. 2. Actors--United States--Biography--Juvenile literature. I. Title.
791.4302/8092--dc22
[B]

2012946490

Jennifer Lawrence

Contents

Rising Star

Jennifer plays Katniss Everdeen in The Hunger Games movies.

Jennifer Lawrence is a talented actress. She has appeared in popular movies. She is best known for starring in movies based on The Hunger Games book **series**.

Family Ties

Jennifer Shrader Lawrence was born in Louisville, Kentucky, on August 15, 1990. Her parents are Karen and Gary Lawrence. Her older brothers are Ben and Blaine.

As Jennifer grew up, her mom ran a children's camp. Her dad owned a construction business. Jennifer liked horses and sports.

Louisville is a large city on the Ohio River. It is home to a famous horse race called the Kentucky Derby.

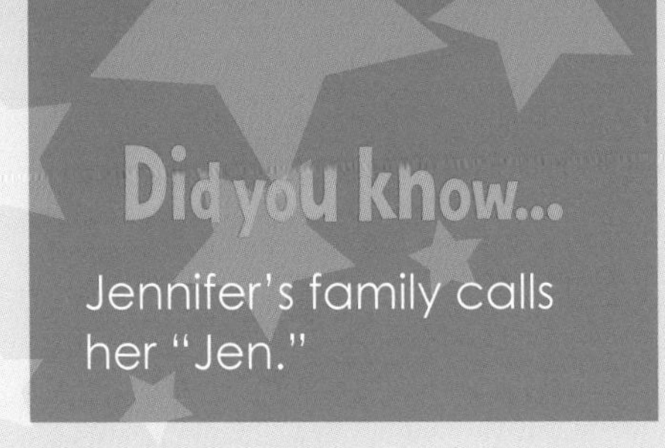

Starting Out

Jennifer began acting when she was very young. As a child, she appeared in church plays. She grew her talents by cheerleading in school. She also acted in local plays.

When Jennifer was 14, she visited New York City, New York, with her mom. There, a talent scout noticed her. He took her picture and shared it with **agents**.

Soon, agents started calling Jennifer. They wanted her to try out for **professional** acting parts!

New York City is home to many talent agencies. Jennifer and her mom were visiting talent agencies when the scout found her.

Did you know...

The Bill Engvall Show is a comedy about a family. Jennifer played Bill's daughter, Lauren, on the show.

Jennifer finished high school early. She moved to New York and became a **professional** actress. She started out by appearing in television **commercials**. She also got small parts on television shows.

Around 2007, Jennifer moved to Los Angeles, California. There, she had a **role** on *The Bill Engvall Show*. Jennifer said she wasn't very good at first. But as she worked regularly, her skills improved.

Jennifer acted on *The Bill Engvall Show* with Graham Patrick Martin (*left*), Bill Engvall (*center back*), and Skyler Gisondo (*center front*).

Lights! Camera! Action!

In 2008, Jennifer began to appear in movies. That year, she acted in *The Poker House*. This was her first starring role! It helped make her a better actress.

Jennifer's next big movie role was in *The Burning Plain*. For this part, she worked with famous actresses Charlize Theron and Kim Basinger. People noticed Jennifer's talent, and she won an award for her work.

In 2008, Jennifer won the Marcello Mastroianni Award. It honored her acting in *The Burning Plain*.

Jennifer wore body paint to play Mystique.

Did you know...

In 2011, Jennifer was nominated for several awards. One of them was the Academy Award for Best Actress for *Winter's Bone*.

Big Break

As Jennifer's talent grew, she landed more **roles**. In 2010, she had an important part in *Winter's Bone*. She starred as a 17-year-old mountain girl who looks after her family.

In 2011, Jennifer acted in a popular action movie called *X-Men: First Class*. She played the character Raven, who is also known as Mystique. This was an exciting part to play!

Hot Ticket

In 2011, Jennifer was excited to be offered her most important **role** yet. She was asked to star as Katniss Everdeen in *The Hunger Games*.

Jennifer liked playing **challenging** parts in movies. But, she took three days before she accepted the role. That was because she knew the movie would make her very famous.

Jennifer colored her hair brown to play Katniss.

In 2011, Jennifer spent many months working on *The Hunger Games*. She had to learn to shoot a bow like her character. The movie was filmed in parts of North Carolina.

In March 2012, *The Hunger Games* opened. Fans were very excited for this movie! It was the first of a four-movie **series** based on books.

Jennifer's costars in *The Hunger Games* were Josh Hutcherson (*left*) and Liam Hemsworth (*right*).

The Hunger Games

The Hunger Games movies are based on a book **series** by Suzanne Collins. The books are popular. So, fans were excited to see the first movie of the series.

The Hunger Games is the story of Katniss Everdeen. It is set in the **future**. At that time, children are forced by the government to fight on television. Katniss and her friend Peeta must work together to stay alive.

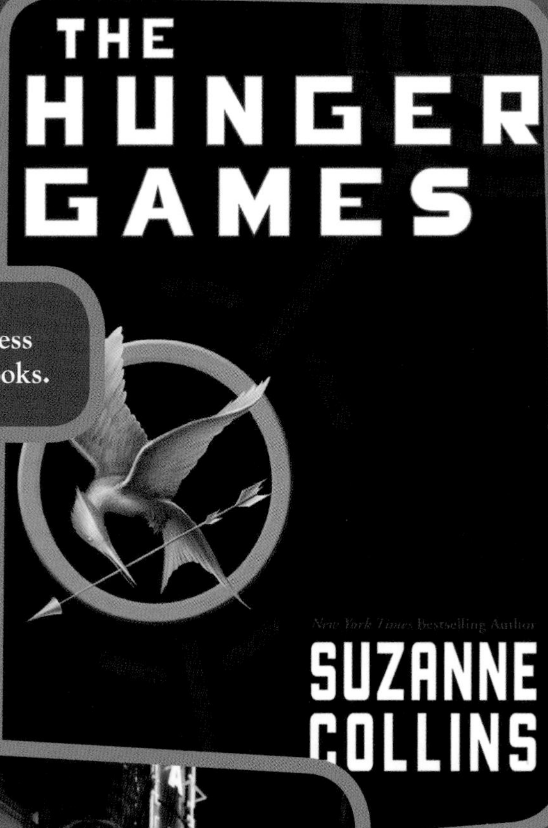

Suzanne (*left*) found success with her Hunger Games books.

When *The Hunger Games* opened, people attended midnight movie showings.

An Actress's Life

As an actress, Jennifer is very busy! She spends time practicing **lines**. For some parts, she must learn special skills. During filming, she works on a movie **set** for several hours each day.

Sometimes Jennifer travels to other states or countries to make movies. She may be away from home for several months.

Jennifer learned archery to play the role of Katniss. She trained with Olympic archer Khatuna Lorig (*left*).

Hunger Games fans often ask Jennifer to sign books and photos.

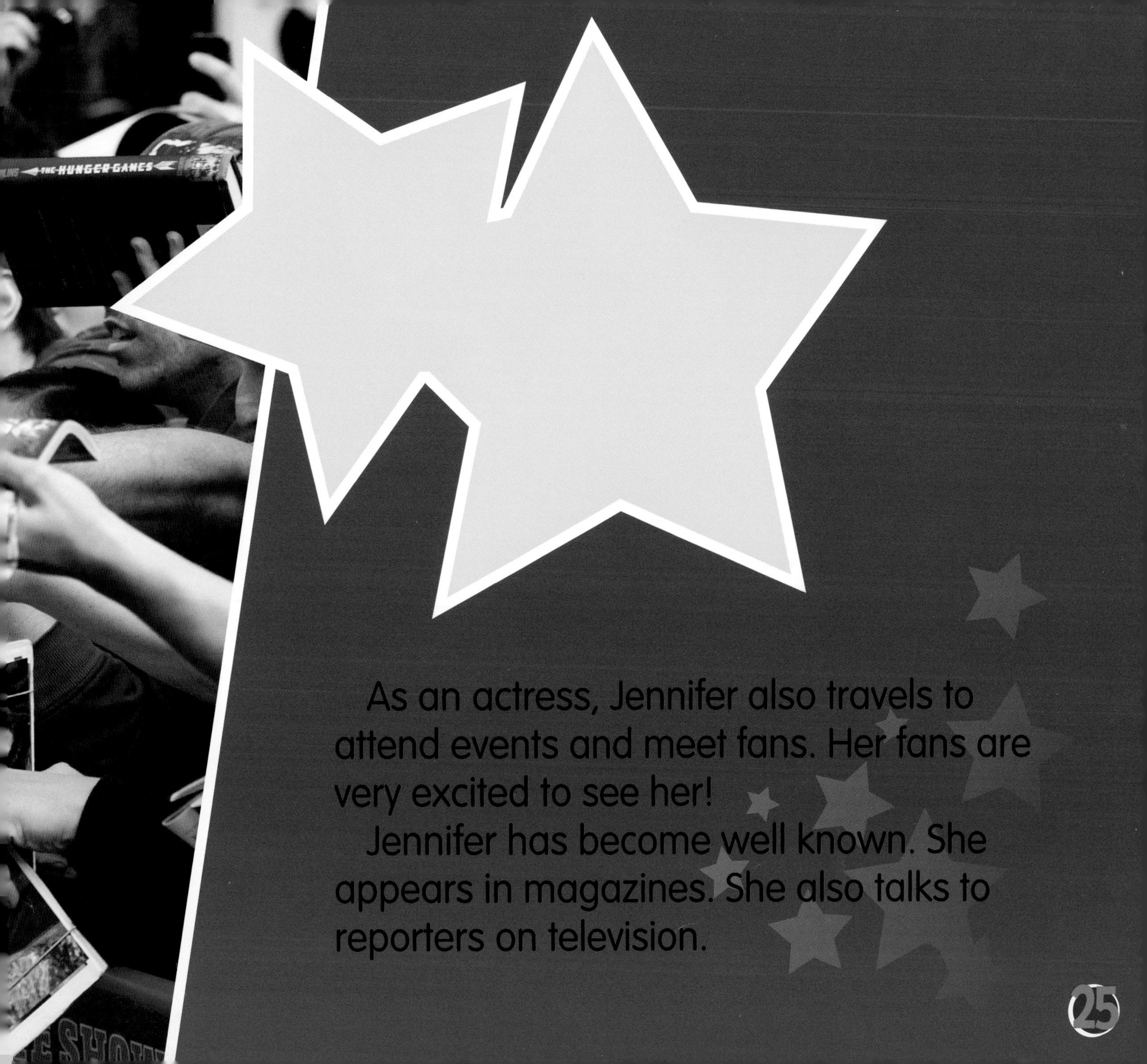

As an actress, Jennifer also travels to attend events and meet fans. Her fans are very excited to see her!

Jennifer has become well known. She appears in magazines. She also talks to reporters on television.

Off the Screen

Jennifer spends her free time at home or visiting her family in Kentucky. She enjoys painting.

Jennifer likes to work with groups that help people in need. Sometimes, she attends events to raise money for certain causes.

Jennifer enjoys going to fashion shows. Sometimes, she visits countries such as France to see them!

Buzz

Jennifer's opportunities continue to grow. In 2012, she began working on the second movie of The Hunger Games **series**. It is called *The Hunger Games: Catching Fire*.

Fans are excited to see what's next for Jennifer Lawrence. Many believe she has a bright **future**!

Reporters often take Jennifer's picture. She dresses up for some events.

Snapshot

★**Name**: Jennifer Shrader Lawrence

★**Birthday**: August 15, 1990

★**Birthplace**: Louisville, Kentucky

★**Appearances**: *The Bill Engvall Show, The Poker House, The Burning Plain, Winter's Bone, X-Men: First Class, The Hunger Games, The Hunger Games: Catching Fire*

Important Words

agent a person who works to help actors get jobs.

challenging (CHA-luhn-jihng) testing one's strengths or abilities.

commercial (kuh-MUHR-shuhl) a short message on television or radio that helps sell a product.

future (FYOO-chuhr) a time that has not yet occurred.

lines the words an actor says in a play, a movie, or a show.

professional (pruh-FEHSH-nuhl) working for money rather than for pleasure.

role a part an actor plays.

series a set of similar things or events in order.

set the place where a movie or a television show is recorded.

Web Sites

To learn more about Jennifer Lawrence, visit ABDO Publishing Company online. Web sites about Jennifer Lawrence are featured on our Book Links page. These links are routinely monitored and updated to provide the most current information available.

www.abdopublishing.com

Index